Stepping Stone

Every step upward is a step closer to your dreams.

Saswat Abhigyanam

Ukiyoto Publishing

All global publishing rights are held by
Ukiyoto Publishing

Published in 2024

ISBN 9789367955291

www.ukiyoto.com

This book is dedicated
To my mama and bapa for everything and much more.
To my Maa & Aja for allowing me to dip in the ocean of their wisdom.
To my Teachers. They showered their rain of knowledge on me when I was a bud so that I blossomed and become a beautiful flower.
To the one who makes my heart soar the galaxy and beyond.
And to all readers of my book.

Contents

Chapter 1 The Arrival: Dreams & determination

I, Subham, hail from a small village in Odisha, where dreams are often clouded by the harsh realities of rural life. Yet, I dared to dream big - of becoming a doctor. March had arrived, and the scorching sun seemed to intensify my determination. But, like a stormy cloud, doubts loomed over me. What if I failed? What if I couldn't afford it?

After completing my Class 12 exams, I knew the next step was to prepare for NEET UG. But, finding the right coaching institute was a daunting task for my father and me. It was like searching for a needle in a haystack. We searched far and wide, seeking advice from numerous students, before finally settling on Aakash Institute at Bhubaneswar.

However, the cost of coaching was a significant hurdle. The total fee was approximately three lakhs, broken down into three instalments of forty thousand each, plus an additional nine thousand seven hundred per month for hostel fees. It was a staggering amount for my family to afford. Despite this, I was determined to pursue my dream as I was confident about my abilities.

Although my Class 12 results were yet to be declared, I began preparing for my NEET UG coaching. The schedule was set for May 6th of the following year, and I decided to move from my hometown, Baripada, to Bhubaneswar. I asked my father to rent a car to drop me off at the college with all my belongings, as Bhubaneswar was a new city for me, full of traffic and unfamiliar faces. I wanted to make a good impression, showing that my family could afford a car, even though it was a stretch for us. It was difficult for me to ask my father, but eventually, he agreed.

My parents and I arrived in Bhubaneswar around 9 AM. As we arrived at the center, my eyes widened in awe. The building was imposing, with gleaming glass and steel facades. The reception area was bustling with students and parents, all eager to secure a seat in the prestigious coaching center.

My father took my hand, and we approached the admission counter. The manager, a stern-looking woman with a kind smile, greeted us warmly. "Welcome, young man," she said, looking at me. "We are glad you have chosen our coaching center. We will do our best to help you achieve your dreams.

As I filled the admission forms, my mind began to wander again. I thought about my childhood, about the countless hours I had spent playing doctor-patient with my mother. I had always dreamed of becoming a doctor, of helping people and making a difference in their lives.

The admission process took about an hour or two. During that time, I saw the pain in my father's eyes as he paid the forty thousand rupees. He said, 'तू कर लेगा ना?' which means 'Can you do it?' It was as if he was questioning whether I could really make the most of this expensive coaching and make him proud. I remembered the words of my grandmother, "Believe you can, and you're halfway there." I believed in myself, and that's all that matted at that time.

As the admission process was completed, the manager handed me a welcome kit, complete with books, a bag, and an ID card. "Congratulations, young man," she said, smiling. "You are now a part of our coaching center family.

My mother's eyes filled with tears as she looked at me, her heart swelling with pride. She remembered the day I was born, the way she had held me in his arms and vowed to give me the best possible life. And now, as she looked at his son, she knew that she had done something right.

My father, sensing Mama's emotions, looked up at her, his eyes shining with love and gratitude. And they knew that I would do everything to make them proud.

After completing the admission process at the coaching institute, my parents and I set out to find a hostel for me. We walked to the hostel office, which was about a kilometer away from the institute. After exploring various options, we found a decent hostel, Adarsh Hostel and I was enrolled there. It was a relief to have a comfortable and secure place to stay, allowing me to focus on my studies.

But now it was time for my mother to bid me farewell. She came to my hostel room, AC-3, situated on the third floor. My father had opted for the air-conditioned room, saying, 'I'm already spending around two lakhs on your coaching, why not spend a little more for your comfort?' especially since the summer in Bhubaneswar was scorching hot, with temperatures reaching 45 degrees.

When my mom entered my room, she helped me organize my belongings and tidy up my space. She assisted me in sorting out my books and making my bed, creating a cozy and inviting atmosphere for me to rest. I was exhausted, and her thoughtful gestures allowed me to unwind and recharge. As she was about to leave, my mom offered words of encouragement, saying, 'You will definitely do it! Just focus on your goal, and you can achieve it.' Her unwavering support and belief in me meant the world, and I felt a surge of determination and motivation to work towards my dreams.

As we said our goodbyes, I could see the tears in my mother's eyes. She was crying, and I felt helpless, stuck in that moment, not knowing what to do. It was the first time I was staying away from my family, and a mix of emotions swirled inside me. But eventually, the day came to an end, and I began my new journey, away from home.

Chapter 2 The Hostel Diaries: Unlocked memories

The first day in my hostel was a memorable one. After my parents left me at the hostel, I was left alone, feeling a mix of emotions. It was my first time away from home, and the sudden independence was both exciting and intimidating. I was terrified. Staying alone for the first time, without my parents, was a daunting experience. I felt lost and unsure of what to do. To be honest, it was difficult for me to come to terms with this new reality.

As I sat in my room alone, surrounded by my books and notes, I felt a sense of purpose. I knew that this was just the beginning of my journey, and I was ready to face whatever challenges came my way. I was determined to make my family proud, to make my hometown proud, and more importantly to make myself proud.

My hostel room was a three-bedded AC room, and I was the second person to arrive. My friend, Bhagya who was also from my hometown but had done his schooling in Bhubaneswar, was already there. We quickly became friends, but since he had a morning shift and I had a second shift, we didn't get to spend much time together.

My third roommate, deepak, arrived later that day, and we had a bit of a discussion about who would take which bed. After a friendly argument, we decided that I would take the bed near the wall, my friend Bhagya would take the other bed near the wall, and Deepak would take the middle bed.

Along with my friends, I went to the market to purchase some new books and notes. Meanwhile, my friend suggested to visit the Ram Mandir to seek the lord's blessings before embarking on our journey tomorrow. So we decided to make a quick stop at the temple before heading to the market. We boarded the newly launched MO bus, which conveniently stopped near the Ram Mandir. We got off the bus, bought some flowers, prasad and diyas, and entered the temple. We spent a few hours at the Ram Mandir, waiting in line as it was quite long. After seeking the lord's blessings for our upcoming journey, we returned to our usual schedule and headed out to purchase books and notes.

Although the institute had already provided us with study materials, we wanted to buy some additional MCQ-oriented books to help us prepare better. Little did I know, our institute would teach us line by line, and we would be required to write our own notes verbatim from the handwritten notes provided. I learned this from YouTube and other sources, and seniors confirmed that we would need to purchase those copies before the start of class. I didn't want to miss out on any important notes, and seniors advised me that these handwritten notes were highly valuable since almost all exam questions would come from them. I was determined to capture every detail and make the most of this learning opportunity.

I decided to prepare notes for four subjects - physics, chemistry, zoology, and botany. I bought eight copies, two for each subject. After that, my friends and I went to a nearby hotel, dalma to enjoy some evening snacks, including dosas. We shared stories about our journeys and our common goal of becoming doctors. It was a wonderful time of bonding and motivation!

While returning from the shop, I ran into a few new faces who were also staying in the same hostel. We struck up a conversation and introduced ourselves. We quickly discovered that we had a lot in common and shared similar interests. Before long, we became fast friends and started sharing our experiences and supporting each other. It was wonderful to find a sense of community and connection with others who were going through similar experiences. We deciding to start our journey together from the next day.

On the night of our first day, my roommate and I decided to treat ourselves to a pizza party! We ordered a delicious pie online and shared it, savoring the flavorful start to our new journey together. With full bellies and high spirits, we were eager to dive into our studies, knowing that the upcoming year would be a whirlwind of hard work and dedication. Little did we know, fate had some surprises in store for us!

After the pizza night, I settled in for the evening, and around 10:30 PM, my phone rang. It was my mom calling to check in on my day. I shared with her the challenges I faced and how I was feeling a bit overwhelmed. I opened up to her about my first day in the hostel, and how everything felt new and daunting. We had a brief but comforting conversation, and I could sense her love and support even from afar. Feeling grateful for her call, I drifted off to sleep that night, ready to face the next day with renewed energy and determination.

Chapter 3 Day 1: The Journey Begins

My morning started at 7:00 AM that day, thanks to one of my roommates. Since his class was at 7:00 AM, he set his alarm for 6:00 AM, which unexpectedly woke me up at the same time. As he got ready to leave for his morning class, I was forced to wake up too.

That morning, after waking up, I brushed my teeth, had two biscuits, and started reading. Since my class hadn't begun yet, I took the opportunity to review my biology textbook. I opened my book and started reading Chapter 16: Digestion and Absorption.

Seeing me reading, my friend who was sleeping next to me woke up inside her blanket and also started to read. She was inspired by my studying and decided to join in.

Around 9:00 AM, while we were reading, my friend Deepak suggested me lets have some breakfast. So, we headed to the hostel canteen. Since it was Monday, idlis were served with sambar and chutney. Although I'm not a fan of idlis in the morning, I didn't have any other option, so I reluctantly ate the idli. After breakfast, I returned to my study table to continue reading.

Then, I called my mom and asked how her night was. She asked about mine, and I shared that I couldn't sleep, just tossing and turning in bed. To be honest, it was my first time staying away from my parents and home, and I was feeling homesick. I kept thinking about home and found it difficult to sleep. I shared all this with my mom, and she reassured me, saying, 'You'll get accustomed soon, don't worry. It's normal. You've gone for a mission, go and conquer it!'

As the day went on, it was time for lunch. After lunch, around 2:00 PM, I prepared for my evening class. In the meantime, my roommate Bhagya, who had a 7:00 AM morning shift class, returned. I asked him about his day and what he learned in his morning class. He shared his notes with me, and I quickly reviewed them to get an idea of what was covered. Then, I got ready for my afternoon class, which started at 3:00 PM.

My evening class starts at 3:15 PM, typically beginning with a daily test that lasts 45 minutes. However, since it was my first class, the daily test was not conducted. After that, our normal classes began at 4:00 PM, running till 9:15 PM, covering four subjects, each with a one-hour lecture and a 15-minute break in between.

On my first day in class, I met a number of new students, including some who were repeat students (also known as 'droppers'). A few of them were three-year droppers, meaning they had taken three years of coaching before joining this class again.

As it was my first day, I always wanted to sit in the front bench. My roommate Deepak and I chose seats in the front row. We were also welcomed by another student named Swagat from Balasore, who was sitting nearby.

In the first class, we were taught the basics of all the subjects. In physics, we started with 'The Physical World,' which is a topic that usually has only one or two questions in the NEET UG exam. We were taught by PVC Sir. He is also one of the decent faculty members in physics. After that, our chemistry class was taken by one of the most popular faculties in Bhubaneswar, CMN Sir. He is indeed a gem in chemistry! My first encounter with CMN sir left a lasting impression. He walked in, a medium-built man with an aura of confidence, and introduced himself with a warm 'hello.' As our chemistry faculty, he assured us that he'd guide us in becoming proficient doctors. CMN sir has a unique gift for motivating each student. Although he's known to be strict, his vast knowledge of chemistry makes him unparalleled. His teaching style is a perfect blend of challenge and inspiration. On the first day, he asked each of us to introduce ourselves and share why we wanted to become doctors. When it was my turn, I confidently shared my passion for helping others and making a positive impact on people's lives. CMN sir listened intently, and with a hint of humor, he teased me, saying, 'So, you don't want money?' The class chuckled, but then he turned serious and said, 'Jokes apart, you will be a good doctor.'

Coming to zoology and Botany, zoology is taught by ZRR Sir. He's one of the funniest guys I've ever seen in my life! Although he's quite capable, he knows how to make the class more enjoyable and engaging. After zoology, we have Botany, taught by a tall, young, and energetic man, BRS Sir. He's from Bihar and started teaching us the basics of Botany, The Living World.

The first day was truly great for me, and it's a memory I'll cherish. I met many new students, some of whom were in similar situations as me, having just completed their 12th standard. Others were repeat students, including one-year droppers, two-year repeaters, and three-year repeaters. As we started interacting, we soon created a WhatsApp group among all of us, which helped us connect and communicate more easily. The senior repeaters were really helpful and supportive. They offered valuable suggestions on how to study effectively, how to stay competitive, and how to manage our time. They shared their own experiences and insights, which were truly enlightening. As my first day in the coaching institute comes to a close, I'd like to end with a quote that resonated with me...

The journey of a thousand miles starts with a single step.

Chapter 4 Laughter and Learning: A Memorable Night with Seniors

As the days went by, I started to settle into the hostel routine. One night, a few seniors came to our room and introduced themselves. I was a bit nervous at first, but they quickly put me at ease with their warm smiles and friendly demeanor. It was a friendly and healthy interaction, not ragging at all! They shared valuable advice and suggestions, which was really helpful. They told us about things we should do and what to expect, which made us feel more comfortable and prepared.

They asked us about our interests and hobbies, and we chatted about everything from movies to sports.

One of them, a tall and lanky guy named Kamlakanta bhai, gave me some valuable advice. "Don't stress too much about studies," he said. "Make sure you take time for yourself and enjoy the hostel life. It's a once-in-a-lifetime experience."

Another senior, Sarthak bhai shared his own experiences. "Don't be afraid to ask for help," he said. The teachers and seniors are always willing to support you. And don't hesitate to speak up if you face any problems.

Kamalakanta bhai highlighted the importance of the NCERT text book in scoring good marks. At first, I didn't understand what he meant to say, but later I realized the significance of his advice. He explained that the giving regular review test is a crucial resource that helps us familiarize ourselves with the exam format, question types, and time management. He also stressed the importance of solving MCQs and previous year's questions, emphasizing that it's crucial to prepare with at least twenty test series. This, he explained, will not only help us familiarize ourselves with the exam format and question types but also aid in time management.

He highlighted the significance of time management in scoring well in the NEET exam, as well as in learning and revising topics efficiently. He pointed out that previous years' frequently asked topics are often repeated, so it's essential to focus on those areas. By doing so, we can optimize our preparation and make the most of our study time.

He also emphasized that the notes provided by the faculties are among the best resources available, and that all the exam questions will be sourced from those notes. He stressed that to score well, we need to thoroughly memorize and understand the notes, as they cover all the essential concepts and topics. He advised us to focus on mastering the notes, rather than trying to study from multiple sources, as the notes are tailored to the exam format and question types.

Rahul bhai also emphasized the importance of honesty with oneself, particularly in review tests or AITS. He stressed that it's not about the score itself, but about the integrity and authenticity of one's own performance. He cautioned against cheating or resorting to shortcuts, emphasizing that a lower score earned honestly is far more valuable than a high score achieved through dishonest means. He encouraged us to focus on our own progress and growth, rather than comparing ourselves to others or trying to impress anyone else. 'Your score should be your own, not anyone else's,' he said, driving home the point that integrity and self-awareness are essential for true success.

As we chatted, they offered some more valuable advice about navigating hostel life, from managing our time effectively to dealing with homesickness. We started talking about our interests, hobbies, and backgrounds. They shared some amazing stories about their own experiences in the hostel, from late-night pizza parties to memorable sports matches. We laughed and joked together, and I felt like I'd known them for years.

One of them, Partha Bhai pulled out his guitar and started strumming a few chords. We had an impromptu jam session, singing along to our favorite songs. It was an incredible feeling, bonding with my new friends over music.

There I realized that I had been making a mistake by trying to study from multiple sources, and that the faculties' notes and NCERT are indeed a treasure trove of knowledge. As they left my room, I felt an overwhelming sense of gratitude. I realized I was fortunate to be surrounded by such kind and supportive individuals. Their guidance extended beyond my immediate needs in UG coaching; I knew that some of them would become exceptional doctors and lifelong mentors. I felt blessed to have them in my life, and I looked forward to learning from them and growing together. That night I felt a sense of belonging and connection with my new hostel family.

Chapter 5 Lost in the Coaching Maze

Soon, life became monotonous, as it often does, everywhere. Faculties came and went, teaching and leaving. The initial joy and excitement of the first day slowly faded away, replaced by a grueling schedule. We were forced to attend classes, and the daily tests became a source of stress and anxiety. The pressure to perform well and keep up with the pace was mounting.

As time passed, I met some wonderful friends, including Ankita. We quickly became very close friends and started sharing our study schedules. We read together, discussed topics, and became great study partners. Ankita was a huge help to me, and I also tried my best to assist her in solving physics doubts. We supported each other, and our friendship grew stronger. We encouraged each other to stay focused and motivated, making our study sessions more productive and enjoyable.

It had been almost a month since we started at the coaching institute, and the daily routine was beginning to feel repetitive and dull. The initial excitement has worn off, and I was no longer the center of attention. The faculties seem to have lost interest in me, and I was not receiving the same level of guidance and support as I was getting when I first started. It feels like they're prioritizing the repeaters and high-scoring students, leaving me freshers feeling neglected and overlooked.

Not only was I struggling academically, but even getting a seat in the front bench had become a nightmare. Everyone was competing for those coveted seats, and it felt like a race. To secure a spot, we had to arrive a full hour before the class started, which was exhausting. The class begins at 3.15 pm, but we had to be there by 2 pm to have any hope of getting a front-row seat. It was like the stress was piling up, and I couldn't catch a break.

The worst part was yet to come. About a month or two into our coaching classes, the Class 12 results were declared. I was on edge, waiting to hear from my dad, who called me with the news. I wasn't prepared for what he told me - it was one of the darkest nights for me. I had been expecting decent marks, but my math score was a huge let-down. I had scored 91% in Biology, 93% in Chemistry, and 95% in Physics, but my math mark was a disappointment. I felt like I had fallen short, and the stress was overwhelming.

The disappointment of my class XII results felt like déjà vu. I had experienced a similar letdown in class X when I was expecting a CGPA of 10 but got 9.8 instead. The same feelings of frustration and disappointment flooded my mind, making it hard for me to sleep that night. Memories of my class X journey came rushing back – the hard work, late-night studies for the board exam, and everything that had seemed so crucial at the time. It felt like all my efforts had been in vain, and I couldn’t help but wonder if I was repeating the same pattern again.

The next week brought another challenge. The NEET results were declared, and I was nervous but hopeful. However, my score was a huge disappointment - 282 marks out of 720. I had taken the exam without any coaching, relying solely on my Class XII preparation. I felt like I had let myself down, and the emotions were overwhelming. I remember crying on the phone with my mom and dad, feeling lost and uncertain about my future. But they were calming and supportive, telling me this too shall pass. They reminded me to focus on the present and that I had the potential to improve and score better next time.

As I sat in my room, staring blankly at my books, my friend Ankita called me. "Hey, how's it going? I've been noticing that you've been struggling a lot lately."

I sighed, feeling a bit overwhelmed. "I just can't seem to catch up. I'm falling behind in class, and I don't know how to get back on track."

Ankita listened patiently, then offered some words of encouragement. "You're not alone, okay? We're all struggling. But you can't give up. You have to keep pushing forward."

I nodded, feeling a small sense of determination. "You're right. I just need to focus and work harder."

Even fifteen days after the results, I couldn't shake off the feeling of disappointment and guilt. I was constantly thinking about the past, replaying what I could have done differently to improve my scores. I felt like I had let myself and my parents down. I started questioning whether I was doing justice to the coaching and resources I had received. I even struggled to eat and drink properly, as my mind was consumed by negative thoughts.

The food situation in the hostel has become a nightmare for everyone. The quality of food, which was decent two months ago, has drastically changed for the worse. What was once tolerable is now a struggle to consume. Even eating a single spoonful of rice has become a challenge. To make matters worse, the curry lacks the essential ingredient – dal – and is instead filled with water. This subpar food quality has added to my already heightened tension and stress levels day by day, and it's becoming unbearable.

Additionally, the pocket money I receive from my parents is barely sufficient, making it difficult to manage my expenses. However, I feel hesitant to ask for more, considering they already pay a substantial amount of ₹9,700 per month for my hostel fees and ₹1,00,000 for my coaching. Furthermore, I've consistently failed to meet their expectations since class X, making it even harder for me to request extra money. As a result, I have to make do with the amount they provide and find ways to stretch it further.

All these issues started to affect my performance in class. Two months ago, I was consistently scoring high marks in daily tests, but now my results have started to suffer. My marks have decreased, and I've fallen behind on my work, creating a massive backlog. I feel hopeless and helpless, unsure of how to catch up and overcome this challenges.

In addition to my academic struggles, I was also having disagreements with my roommate over minor issues. We would argue about switching on or off the fan, light, or studying at night. For instance, if I wanted to study late at night, he would want to sleep early and vice versa. These small disagreements accumulated and created a lot of tension and frustration between us. It was like the pressure was building up, and we couldn't seem to find a way to resolve our differences.

Despite having disagreements and fought over small things, but one rainy day incident brought us closer together. We had ordered food from sizzler hotel, but due to the rain, we had to collect it ourselves. The three of us ventured out, braved the heavy rain, and collected the food. When we reached our hostel, we found water inside our food packets, which made us burst out laughing. We warmed up the food and shared it from a single plate, showing that despite our disagreements, we cared about each other. That moment, we realized that our bond was stronger than our petty fights.

As the sun began to set on another long day of studying, my phone rang, breaking the silence. It was my granny's voice on the other end, warm and loving as always.

"How are you, Bacha" she asked, her voice filled with concern.

"I'm doing okay, Maa," I replied, trying to sound brave. "Just studying a lot."

My granny's voice was like a balm to my soul. She asked me about my preparation, "Fuku, how's your studying going? Are you able to understand everything in class?"

I replied, "Yes, Maa, I'm trying my best. But sometimes I feel like I'm falling behind. The classes are so long and the teachers are always giving us so much homework."

My granny listened attentively, then asked, "And how are your teachers? Are they helping you with your doubts?"

I thought for a moment before responding, "Most of them are okay, Maa. But there are some chapters which are really tough. I couldn't understand things very well, and I always feel lost in his class."

My granny made a sympathetic noise, then asked, "And what about your friends, beta? Are you making friends in your classes?"

I smiled, feeling a bit more positive. "Yes, Maa, I've made a few friends. We study together and help each other out when we're struggling."

My granny's voice was warm with approval. "That's great, Fuku. Having good friends can make all the difference. Just remember to stay focused and keep working hard. You'll do great things, I just know it."

"Bacha, don't worry," she said, her voice filled with reassurance. "You are doing your best, and that's all that matters. We are all proud of you, no matter what."

Then, my mother's sister, Aunty, got on the phone. "Doctor babu , how's your food? Are you eating well?"

"Yes, Aunty, the food is okay," I replied. "I'm managing."

My cousin, Sidhu, who was also on the phone, chimed in. "Bhaiya, what's your daily routine like? Do you get any time to relax?"

"I try to study for at least 8-10 hours a day," I replied. "But sometimes it's hard to focus, and I get distracted."

My Nana, Mamu, got on the phone next. "Beta, don't worry about the distractions," he said. "Just focus on your goals, and you'll get there."

As I listened to my family's voices, I felt a sense of comfort and reassurance. I knew that they were all rooting for me, and that gave me the strength to keep going.

As we talked, my Nana asked, "Beta, when do you think you'll be able to come home?"

"I'm not sure, Nana," I replied. "I have a lot of studying to do before my exams."

My family understood, and we talked for a while longer before saying our goodbyes.

As I hung up the phone, I felt a sense of peace wash over me. I knew that I wasn't alone in this journey. I had my family's love and support to carry me through.

My oldest stress reliever has been coffee. Having a sip of coffee in the evening has become a constant source of comfort. In fact, coffee and tea have become my constant companions throughout my preparation. My day starts with coffee, and my night ends with coffee. It's helped me stay awake and focused during long study sessions, allowing me to push through the night. As tension and stress built up, coffee became my go-to solution to alleviate all the anxiety. It's almost as if coffee has become an essential fuel for my studies, helping me power through the challenges and stay on track.

Thanks to and family members, friends and seniors, they helped me a lot to cover the backlog, but despite their support, I still felt like I was lagging behind. It was a challenging time, and I struggled to keep up with the pace.

Chapter 6 The Self - doubt Trap

Months after our busy schedule, my roommate and I with my friend Swet finally found some time to explore the streets of Bhubaneswar. As it was my first time in the city, which is the capital of Odisha, I was unfamiliar with the names of the roads and places. Luckily, one of my roommates, Bhagya, who is from my native place but did his schooling in Bhubaneswar, offered to help us navigate the city. He promised to show us around and help us get to know the place better. Along with Deepak, we set out to discover the wonders of Bhubaneswar, and I was excited to see what this new city had in store for us!

The only guidance my father gave me was about the route to my institute. He told me that it starts from Vani Vihar, then comes Acharya Vihar, and finally, Jaydev Vihar. He instructed me to get down at Acharya Vihar, which was my stop, and from there, I had to make my way to Aakash Institute. That's all I knew about Bhubaneswar at that time.

On that day, I and my friends visited the Ram Mandir, one of the largest temples in Bhubaneswar. Afterwards, we headed to the Lingaraj Temple and explored a few other places. We also stopped by some of the biggest malls in the city, including the Esplanade One mall.

After a fun-filled day of sightseeing and exploration, we finally ended our journey that day.

We wrapped up the day with a delicious dinner at the Sizzler Restaurant, which was conveniently located near our hostel. It was the perfect way to cap off an eventful day, sharing laughter and stories over a sizzling hot meal with my friends.

We also had the opportunity to explore the Mo Bus, a government initiative for public transportation in Odisha that had recently launched at that time. We were impressed by how convenient and affordable it was – the fares were incredibly low! We thoroughly enjoyed our ride on the Mo Bus and appreciated the ease it offered for getting around the city.

Three months passed, and I was in a state of confusion, wondering if I was studying the right way. Late-night conversations with friends and procrastination only added to my distress. I felt lost and uncertain about my academic path, and the procrastination habit was significantly affecting my progress.

The fact that my friends were playing PUBG at that time was an additional temptation. I started playing with them, and it drastically affected my focus. Despite having evening classes, I would join the late-night gaming sessions, which would go on till 1 o'clock. We would start playing at 10 PM, and it would disrupt my study routine. The online gaming significantly impacted my academic performance during that time.

In addition to the gaming distraction, I was also feeling like the coaching wasn't helping me as much as I had hoped. I was starting to feel like a burden, just going through the motions. The initial days of motivation and excitement had worn off, and I was feeling discouraged. The coaching that was supposed to help me improve my studies was now feeling like a chore.

The boy who was once reading for 8 hours a day in the initial days is now struggling to read for even 2-3 hours a day. It's like the spark that drove him to study with such dedication has faded, and he's finding it difficult to muster the same enthusiasm and focus.

My life has become a mountainous challenge. Everything seems to be tearing apart, and I'm lost. I don't know what to do or how to move forward. I'm just waking up, attending classes, and returning home, feeling like I'm stuck in a never-ending cycle. Life has become a hellish struggle, and I feel like I have no one to turn to for support.

The never-ending cycle was consuming me, but then I discovered a new web series called 'The Kota Factory' that sparked some inspiration. It was like a breath of fresh air, offering a glimmer of hope and motivation to break free from the monotony.

The review test was approaching, but I hadn't studied for the last 15 days. Although I had studied initially, I felt like I hadn't read anything. However, just two days before the exam, I felt fairly prepared after intensively reviewing the material. I had read the NCERT line by line, expecting to score a decent amount. But to my surprise, the questions in the review test were completely off-syllabus! They were extremely difficult, the kind of questions that are rarely asked in the NEET entrance exam. I felt frustrated and demoralized, thinking that despite putting in so much effort, I wouldn't be able to score well.

The accumulation of frustrations was taking a toll on me. The boy who once liked the subjects now hated them after reading so much, yet still not scoring well. It was disheartening to see my friends and seniors performing well, while I was left feeling clueless about what to do. The gap between my efforts and results seemed to be growing, and it was hard to cope with the disappointment.

After the review test results, I noticed a change in the teachers who were once very kind and helpful to me. They seemed to have lost interest in supporting me, and started ignoring my doubts and questions. I felt like I was being judged solely on my performance, and that my worth as a student was tied to my test scores. It was disheartening to feel like I couldn't ask questions or seek help because of my poor marks.

The teachers' focus was solely on the first two or three benches, leaving the rest of us feeling neglected. They seemed oblivious to what was happening in the last seven or eight benches. My goal was always to sit in the first or second bench, but it was getting increasingly difficult day by day. I felt like I was missing out on important instruction and guidance because of where I was seated.

Everything changed when my marks slipped. Friends who once saw me as a top performer now view me as a poor performer. It's like I've lost my identity and reputation. Things aren't going well for me, and I don't know how to cope with this new dynamic. I feel like I'm losing myself and my confidence.

However, I found solace in playing PUBG. Playing games from 10 pm to 1 am was my way of relaxing and unwinding. After a long and hectic day, playing PUBG for three to four hours was like heaven. It was my escape from the frustrations and stresses that had built up. Gaming became my go-to relaxation technique, helping me temporarily forget about my worries and recharge.

However, I knew that gaming was affecting me negatively day by day. When the second review test results came out, my marks were even lower than the first review test. It was like I was mentally deteriorating, and my academic performance was suffering. I felt like I was losing control, and my gaming habit was taking a toll on my mental health.

The coaching institution that initially promised to support me from the grassroots level has changed over time. They no longer give me the attention and importance they once did. In fact, I feel like they've lost interest altogether. I'm not the only one who's experienced this; many other students have faced similar struggles. It's disappointing and frustrating to see the lack of support from an institution that was supposed to help us grow and succeed.

What's even more alarming is that some of my friends, who were once genuinely good at academics and passionate about learning, have now turned to alcohol and smoking. I was taken aback by this transformation, as it's not something I'm used to seeing. Being away from home and in a new environment has exposed me to things I've never encountered before. It's disheartening to see my friends, who had so much potential, succumb to these unhealthy habits.

One night after my classes over I walked out of the coaching center, feeling demotivated and defeated, I slowly made my way down the stairs. Lost in my thoughts, I didn't notice the person standing in front of me until I almost collided with him.

It was CMN Sir, my Chemistry teacher. He looked at me with concern and asked, "How are you doing? How's your preparation going?"

I hesitated, feeling a bit embarrassed. "It's...it's going okay, Sir. I'm trying my best."

CMN Sir looked at me with concern. "You know, I've noticed that you haven't been asking many questions in class lately. Is everything okay? Are you facing any difficulties?"

I shook my head, feeling a bit ashamed. "No, Sir. I'm just...I don't know, I feel like I'm not understanding things as well as I should be."

CMN Sir nodded thoughtfully. "I see. Well, let me tell you something. Your parents are investing a huge amount of money in your education, and you're investing your precious years. Don't waste this opportunity. Try to prepare well and get into a good medical college. You have the potential, but you need to believe in yourself and work hard."

I felt a surge of motivation at his words. "Thank you, Sir. I'll try my best."

CMN Sir smiled and patted me on the back. "I know you will. Just remember, it's not just about the marks you score, it's about the effort you put in and the person you become in the process."

I felt a surge of motivation at his words. I decided to sit down and study, determined to make the most of my time.

I sat down at my desk, opened my books, and began to read. But as I sat there, I couldn't shake the feeling of restlessness. My mind kept wandering, and I found myself thinking about the game I had played the night before.

Just as I was trying to focus, my neighbor from the next room called out to me. "Hey, dude! Want to play a game?"

I hesitated, feeling a pang of guilt. I had just promised myself that I would study, but the temptation of the game was too strong.

"Yeah, sure," I said, closing my books and standing up.

My friend grinned. "Dude, you're really good at this game. You should consider going pro."

I laughed. "I don't think so. I need to focus on my studies, not gaming."

But my friend persisted. "Come on, it'll be fun. And who knows, you might even be able to make a career out of it."

I shook my head. "I don't think my parents would be too happy about that. They're already worried about my studies."

My friend nodded understandingly. "Yeah, I get it. But just think about it, okay? It could be a way out of this stressful life we're living."

I nodded, but I knew I couldn't let gaming become a distraction from my studies. I needed to stay focused and motivated if I was going to achieve my goals.

Time flies like sand slipping through my hands. Before I knew it, Durga Puja was around the corner, and I hadn't visited my home in a while. The seven-day holiday was a welcome break, and I was eager to recharge and start anew. It felt like a long-overdue opportunity to rejuvenate and refresh my mind and spirit.

Before I knew it, Durga Puja was around the corner, and I hadn't visited your home in a while. The seven-day holiday was a welcome break, and I was eager to recharge and start anew. It felt like a long-overdue opportunity to rejuvenate and refresh your mind and spirit.

Chapter 7 Rising from the Ashes

After Durga Puja, I entered the second phase of my journey. During the Puja, I focused on covering my backlog, and I'm happy to say that I was mostly successful in catching up on my studies. It was a productive period for me, and I feel more on top of my work now.

Something remarkable happened - my marks, which were previously poor, started to increase. And then, the All India Test Series began. In my first test series, I scored approximately 450 marks, which was a milestone for me. Crossing the 400-mark barrier for the first time was a thrilling experience, and I felt an immense sense of accomplishment.

The All India Test Series was a beacon of hope for me. I approached it with a determination to learn from my mistakes. I took the exams, analyzed my performance, and revised again and again. Each attempt was an opportunity to grow and improve. I was relentless in my pursuit of excellence, and the test series became a transformative experience for me.

As winter approached, the days grew shorter, and I found myself with less time for my studies. Just when I needed to focus, some of my friends started planning a trip to Bali (बाली यात्रा). I was torn between my desire to join them and my need to prioritize my studies."In the end, I decided to join my friends on the trip to Bali Yatra (बाली यात्रा) , which is being held at Cuttack I'm excited to take a break and explore new places with my friends!

"I'm thinking of joining you on the trip to Bali Yatra," I said to my friend, Swet, seeking his advice.

"Are you sure that's a good idea?" Swet asked, concern etched on his face. "You have your exams coming up soon. Don't you think you should be focusing on your studies?"

"I know, but I really need a break," I replied. "I've been studying non-stop for months, and I'm feeling burnt out. Besides, it's not like I'm going to forget everything I've studied in just a few days."

Swet nodded thoughtfully. "I understand where you're coming from, but just make sure you don't get too distracted, okay?"

"I will, don't worry," I said, smiling.

Bali Yatra is a vibrant festival held in Cuttack, Odisha, celebrating the ancient maritime heritage of the region. Marking the voyages of Odia traders toy Southeast Asia, it features cultural performances, traditional crafts, and a grand fair on the Mahanadi River banks, blending history, culture, and festivity in unique harmony.

When the form came out, I knew it was time to make my preferences clear. I filled out the form and indicated my top choice as Bhubaneswar. Fingers crossed that I get my first preference!

With the form submitted, I had just three months - a mere 90 days - left to prepare for my exam. I knew I had to be focused and disciplined if I wanted to succeed. So, I created a study schedule and dove into my preparation, determined to make the most of the time I had left.

Each day felt like time was flying by, and I wasn't making the most of it. I couldn't believe how quickly the days were passing, and yet, I hadn't prepared as much as I needed to. I felt like I'd wasted so much time playing games and getting distracted, which only added to my stress and anxiety about my upcoming exam.

Despite the challenges I faced, I somehow managed to cover my entire syllabus and feel somewhat prepared for the exam. Then, the day arrived, and I took the paper. It was a huge relief to have made it through!

As I woke up early on the morning of the exam, my phone rang. It was my parents calling to wish me good luck.

"Hello, beta! How are you feeling today?" my mother asked, her voice filled with concern.

"I'm feeling good, Mama. A bit nervous, but I'm ready," I replied, trying to sound confident.

"That's my brave beta! We're all proud of you, no matter what. Just go out there and do your best," my father said, his voice filled with encouragement.

"Thanks, Bapa. Thanks, Mama. Your blessings mean a lot to me," I said, feeling a sense of gratitude.

"We're always with you, beta. Don't forget that. Now go and make us proud!" my mother said, her voice filled with love.

I smiled, feeling a sense of determination. "I will, Mama. Don't worry."

As I hung up the phone, my Roommate came up to me and said, "Hey, all the best for your exam, man! I'm sure you'll do great."

I smiled and thanked him, feeling a sense of appreciation for my friend's support. With a final check of my admit card and water bottle, I headed out of the hostel room to face the day ahead.

After taking the exam, I returned home to await my results, which would be declared after a month. It was a bit of a nerve-wracking wait, but I tried to use this time to unwind and distract myself from exam mode. I'd done my best, and now all I could do was wait patiently!

Chapter 8 Lessons learnt and rebooting

Just as I was waiting for my results, a friend from school called me and asked if I had taken admission anywhere yet. They mentioned they were pursuing BSc and expressed concern that I might not be able to crack the NEET UG exam. Their words added to my already mounting confusion and stress. I started doubting myself and my preparation, wondering if I had made a mistake by not taking admission elsewhere.

My friend Satya called me.

"Hey, have you taken admission anywhere?" my friend asked, their voice laced with concern.

"No, I'm still waiting for my results," I replied, trying to sound confident.

"Oh, okay. I just wanted to check. I've taken admission in BSC Science," they said, their words making me feel even more uncertain.

"I see. That's great! Congratulations," I said, trying to sound genuine.

"Yeah, thanks. I'm really excited. But I'm also a bit worried about you. Are you sure you'll be able to crack the NEET exam?" they asked, their voice filled with concern.

"I...I think so. I've been studying hard and I'm feeling pretty confident," I replied, trying to sound convincing.

"But what if you don't get selected? What will you do then?" they asked, their words striking a chord of fear within me.

"I...I don't know. I haven't really thought about it," I admitted, feeling a sense of uncertainty wash over me.

"Well, you should think about it. You should have a backup plan in place, just in case," they said, their words making me feel even more anxious.

"I'll think about it, okay? Thanks for your concern," I said, trying to sound calm.

"No problem, buddy. I just want to make sure you're okay," they said, their voice filled with genuine concern.

"Thanks, I appreciate it," I said, feeling a sense of gratitude towards my friend.

The conversation with my friend left me feeling even more uncertain and anxious. I couldn't shake off the feeling of doubt that lingered within me.

I couldn't shake off the feeling of uncertainty that lingered long after the call ended. I started wondering if I had made a mistake by not taking admission elsewhere. Was I good enough to crack the NEET exam? Only time would tell.

After my exam, I returned home and had a lengthy conversation with my parents. We discussed various possibilities and uncertainties about my future, including which branch to choose, what to do if I don't get selected, and potential career changes down the line.

"Beta, what's wrong?" my mother asked, concern etched on her face. "You seem a bit distracted."

"I'm just worried about my results, Mama," I replied, feeling a sense of anxiety wash over me.

"Don't worry, beta. You've studied hard and you'll do fine. Just have faith in yourself," my father said, his voice filled with reassurance.

"But what if I don't get selected, Papa?" I asked, my voice filled with doubt.

"Then we'll think about other options, beta. There are many other good colleges and courses out there. We'll explore all our options and find the best one for you," my mother said, her voice filled with calmness.

"But I don't want to settle for anything less, Mama. I want to get into a good medical college," I said, feeling a sense of determination.

"I know, beta. And we'll do everything we can to help you achieve your goal. But we also need to be realistic and think about other options. We'll face whatever comes next together, as a family," my father said, his voice filled with wisdom.

I nodded, feeling a sense of gratitude towards my parents. They always knew just what to say to make me feel better.

"Thanks, Mama. Thanks, Papa. Just talking to you both makes me feel better," I said, feeling a sense of relief wash over me.

My parents smiled and hugged me tightly.

"We're always here for you, beta. No matter what happens, we'll face it together," my mother said, her voice filled with love.

I smiled, feeling a sense of hope and determination. I knew that no matter what happened, my parents would always be there to support me.

During that time, after my return home, I thoroughly enjoyed myself, expecting to score well in the exam. However, when the answer key was released, my expectations took a bit of a hit. Despite the setback, I was still hopeful of scoring around 500 marks, which would be enough to secure a decent government seat.

During my time at home, my mother helped me maintain a great schedule. Every day, I'd wake up and start with green tea and biscuits, followed by lunch at 10 am. In the evenings, I'd have snacks and dinner, and then wind down by watching a movie. In fact, I managed to watch thirty to forty movies in just one month! It was a great way to relax and pass the time while waiting for my exam results.

And then, the results were out. Boom! The face of disappointment stared back at me again. I felt like I was hit with a ton of bricks. I had failed again. I felt completely helpless, like there was nothing I could do to change the outcome. All I could do was sit there, feeling the weight of my disappointment.

Despite putting in countless hours of hard work and making immense efforts, I was only able to score approximately 400 marks. The coaching amount, which was a substantial financial burden, felt like a weight on my shoulders, making the disappointment even more difficult to bear. I couldn't help but feel like I had let myself and others down.

I felt utterly lost and didn't know what to do or where to start again. I was torn between continuing on the same path or changing my direction altogether. It was like I was standing at a crossroads, unsure which way to turn. I was questioning my own abilities and wondering if I should explore a different line of study or career path.

Just then, I received a call from my friend Rajesh, who was ecstatic about scoring 650 marks. He asked about my results, but I felt too disheartened to share my score. I hesitantly told him I got 400 marks, feeling a bit embarrassed. But Rajesh, being the supportive friend he is, quickly tried to lift my spirits. "Don't worry, next time you'll definitely get good marks!" he said, trying to reassure me.

The whole day, I received countless calls from all my friends, and I was getting increasingly frustrated. Finally, I couldn't take it anymore, so I switched off my phone and tossed it aside (figuratively, of course!). I just needed some time to process my emotions and escape the constant reminders of my disappointment.

That day was tough, and we still hadn't eaten or slept. But this time, I was surrounded by my loving family, including my parents. My mom, my rock, was right there with me, offering comfort, guidance, and counsel. She kept reassuring me, saying 'no worries, next time you will definitely do better.' But despite her efforts, I could still see the disappointment etched on my father's face.

In the evening I sat in the darkness of my room, the only sound the heavy beating of my heart, I felt a fierce battle raging within me. My mind was a war zone, with doubts and fears clashing against determination and hope. One voice screamed at me to give up, to accept that I wasn't good enough, that I'd never make it. But another voice, a smaller, quieter one, whispered words of encouragement, urging me to keep going, to push through the pain and the fear.

The two voices wrestled for control, each one fighting to be heard, to be believed. I felt like I was being torn apart, like my very soul was being ripped in two. The darkness seemed to closing in around me, suffocating me.

Just as it seemed like the battle within me was reaching its climax, I heard a faint voice calling out to me.

“Beta, dinner is ready!" my mother's voice echoed through the hallway.

I didn't respond. I couldn't respond. I was too caught up in the turmoil raging within me.

But my mother didn't give up. She walked into my room, the light from the hallway spilling in behind her.

"Beta, what's wrong?" she asked, her voice soft with concern.

I didn't look up. I couldn't look up. I was too ashamed, too defeated.

But my mother didn't need me to look up to know what was wrong. She could see it in the way I was sitting, in the way I was breathing.

She walked over to me and sat down beside me, putting a gentle hand on my shoulder.

"Beta, you are not defined by one exam, one result," she said, her voice firm but gentle. "You are so much more than that. You are strong, capable, and talented. Don't let one setback hold you back."

"Beta, come and eat your dinner," she said, her voice firm but gentle. "We'll talk about this later. You need to keep your strength up."

I slowly got up, feeling like I was moving through quicksand. My mother guided me to the dinner table, where my father was already seated.

As I sat down, my mother placed a plate of food in front of me.I staring blankly at my food, Mama noticed my distress.

"Why are you so upset?" she asked, concern etched on her face.

I sighed, feeling a lump form in my throat. "I just feel like I've failed, Mama. I didn't get the marks I wanted, and now I'm worried that I'll never get into a good medical college."

Mama reached out and took my hand, her touch warm and comforting. "Beta, failure is not the end of the world. It's just a stepping stone to success. You can't give up now."

I looked up at her, feeling a tear roll down my cheek. "But Mama, I feel like I've let you and Papa down. I've wasted a whole year, and now I'm not even sure if I'll get admission anywhere."

Mama's expression turned stern, but her voice was gentle. "Beta, you have not let us down. We are proud of you, no matter what. And as for admission, we'll cross that bridge when we come to it. Right now, let's just focus on the present moment."

I nodded, feeling a small sense of comfort. Mama squeezed my hand.

"Ek baat yaad rakhna, beta," she said. "Success is not just about achieving your goals. It's about the journey, the struggles, the lessons you learn along the way. You are strong, capable, and talented. Don't ever forget that."

I smiled, feeling a sense of gratitude towards Mama. She always knew just what to say to make me feel better.

"Thank you, Mama," I said, my voice barely above a whisper.

Mama smiled and handed me a plate of food. "Now, eat your dinner and don't worry about anything. We'll face whatever comes next together, as a family."

I nodded, taking a bite of my food. For the first time in days, I felt a sense of hope. Maybe, just maybe, everything would work out after all.

Although my parents are trying to be supportive and caring, I can still see the concern etched on their faces. They're worried about me, and I know they're feeling the pain of my mistakes. I feel like I've let them down by wasting a year and not getting admission anywhere. I can sense their disappointment and concern, and it's hard for me to bear. I know they're trying to be strong for me, but I can see the pain in their eyes.

With this mark, I feel like I've lost all hope. I'll never get admission into a medical college, and I haven't even applied to any other colleges for BSC or other courses. I feel like I've got no options left and that I've missed my chance to pursue my dreams. It's a really tough pill to swallow.

A few days later, I got a call from one of my closest friends, Swet. Turns out, he also didn't do well in the exams and scored lower marks than he had hoped for. We started talking and venting about our disappointment, sharing our frustrations and worries. It was a relief to finally have someone to talk to who understood exactly what I was going through.

Hey, my friend Sweat guided me to start again and pursue my coaching. With my parents' support, I decided to give it another try. Initially, I thought about going back to Aakash Institute for coaching, but then I reconsidered and thought about exploring other options.

But then I remembered how the teachers and staff at the coaching institute in Bhubaneswar treated me last time. The way they spoke to me, the way they made me feel... it was all still fresh in my mind. And that's when I decided not to go back. I didn't want to put myself through that again. The thought of going back to that place and facing the same people and the same treatment was just too discouraging.

I took charge of my studies by creating my own schedule and making a habit of reading books again. I started preparing my own schedule, setting goals, and tracking my progress. I also made a conscious effort to develop a reading habit, which helped me stay focused and motivated.

I took the next step towards my goal by ordering the DLP (Distance Learning Program) from Ellen Institute. I'm now studying and learning from the program materials on my own, which is helping me stay focused and motivated. I'm proud of myself for taking the initiative to continue my education and pursue my dreams.

I invested in a new NCERT textbook to help me continue my studies. My old book was worn out, with thousands of underlines, and I couldn't possibly add any more! So, I bought a brand new book and started reading and preparing for my next attempt. I'm excited to dive in and make progress once again.

With my parents' support, I've been consistently reading and studying, but I'd be lying if I said I wasn't feeling frustrated. The truth is, I haven't secured admission anywhere yet, and time is flying by. It's hard not to feel anxious when I see my peers moving forward, and I'm still waiting for my opportunity.

Chapter 9 The Home Strech

Slowly but surely, time has passed, and it's now been almost six months. I've been trying my absolute best, waking up early every morning to study, reading throughout the day, and even pulling late-night study sessions. I've been doing everything I can to improve my understanding and catch up.

Because this is my only chance, my last chance, I'm giving it my all. I can't afford to lose another year, and I've already wasted one year in coaching. So, I'm trying my best, reading NCERT line by line, and leaving no stone unturned. I'm determined to make the most of this opportunity and succeed."

It all started when I realized I needed to work on my time management skills, which were my weakest point in last year's NEET exam. So, I made a conscious effort to improve it this time around. I started by reading NCERT line by line, then moved on to solving MCQs from Errorless Biology, and finally the master the NCERT. For physics and chemistry, I focused on grasping the concepts rather than just mugging up the material. It's been a game-changer!

After putting in a tremendous amount of hard work and dedication, I've finally feels ready to take on the exam this year. I've taken over 30 practice tests, scoring around 500 in each mock paper. It's been a long and challenging journey, but I'm confident that I've prepared well and am ready to give it my best shot.

Honestly, the last nine months have been incredibly tough for me. Every day has been a challenge, from waking up in the morning to completing my tasks at night. During this time, I've had to disconnect from social media and even stopped using WhatsApp to stay focused on my goals. It's been a difficult journey, but I'm proud of myself for staying committed and persevering through the tough times.

It's not always easy to stay on track, and I've definitely gotten distracted at times. But I'm grateful to have my parents, especially my mom, who have been my rock throughout the last nine months. She's kept me guided and focused, even when I felt like giving up. I can't thank her enough for her unwavering support and encouragement. She's the best!

Over the past nine months, I've faced numerous challenges, including mental breakdowns, tears, and feelings of being stuck. There were times when I felt like life had ended, and I didn't know what to do. I even struggled with negative thoughts and feelings of hopelessness. But then, something changed. I found a glimmer of hope, got motivated, and started practicing yoga. Slowly but surely, I began to cope with my emotions and push through the tough times. And now, I've made it through this difficult period and am ready to take on my exam!

As expected, the exam form arrived in December, and I filled it out, waiting anxiously for my admit card. However, it was only released three days before the exam, which added to my stress levels. To make matters worse, my exam center was not in my hometown, and I had to travel 50 kilometers to appear for the exam. Unfortunately, this did affect my performance, and my result was impacted negatively. Despite this, I'm trying to stay positive and focus on what I learned from the experience.

On the exam day, I woke up at 6 am, got ready, and prepared myself for the big day. My exam was scheduled for 10 am, and I had to travel 50 kilometers to reach the exam center in Balashore. My father and I left our hometown together, and my mother also came along to support me. While I entered the exam hall, both my parents waited outside, providing me with moral support and encouragement. Their presence helped calm my nerves, and I felt more focused and determined to do my best.

As I stood outside the exam hall, my brain and heart began to engage in a fierce battle.

"My brain is telling me I can do this," I thought. "I've studied hard, I've prepared well, and I've got the knowledge. I can ace this exam."

But my heart was a different story. It was filled with doubts and fears.

"What if I forget everything?" my heart whispered. "What if I'm not good enough? What if I fail?"

My brain tried to reassure my heart, but it was a tough sell.

"Come on, heart," my brain said. "We've got this. We've studied for months, we've practiced countless mock tests, and we're ready for this."

But my heart was stubborn.

"I don't know, brain," my heart said. "I just feel so unsure. What if we're not good enough?"

The battle between my brain and heart raged on, with neither side willing to give in.

Just as it seemed like my heart was going to win the battle, I remembered something my mom had told me.

"Tu kar lega, beta."

But then I told myself "It's now or never. Give it your all and leave the rest to fate."

I took a deep breath, feeling a surge of confidence.

"You're right, brain," I thought. "We can do this."

With newfound determination, I walked into the exam hall, ready to face whatever lay ahead.

As I entered the exam hall, a flurry of thoughts flooded my mind. I was worried about failing again, and wondered if I'd be able to succeed this time. I thought about the two years I'd already invested, and whether I'd be able to get into a good college with my marks. I was anxious about scoring well, and wondered if I'd be able to reach my target of 550+ marks. All these thoughts were swirling in my head, making me feel nervous and uncertain again and again.

After finding my seat and getting settled, I felt a sense of relief wash over me. I took a sip of water, gazed at the question paper, and began solving the answers. As I worked through the questions, I started to feel more relaxed and focused. Before I knew it, the three-hour exam was over, and it felt like it had flown by in just a few seconds! Time really does fly when you're in the zone.

As I exited the exam hall, I was expecting a sense of relief and pride, but instead, I saw my parents' faces filled with disappointment. I kept asking them what was wrong, but they didn't want to share the news with me. After 10-15 minutes, my mom finally told me that my school friend had committed suicide just before the exam. I was in shock and couldn't believe what I was hearing. It was a devastating moment for me and my family.

When my mom told me that my friend, who was taking coaching in Kota, had committed suicide, I was in shock. I couldn't believe what I was hearing. It was like the earth had been swept from beneath my feet. My friend was a brilliant and bright student, but she couldn't cope with the stress. It's devastating to think that she felt like she had no other option but to take her own life. This is a tragic reminder that we need to prioritize our mental health and well-being, especially during challenging times.

As I sat with my parents, trying to process the news of my friend's suicide, Mama shared some wise words that have stuck with me: "Being successful is not the most important thing in life. What matters most is being a good human being and learning to cope with life's stress.

I looked at her, feeling a mix of emotions. "But Mama, why do students feel so pressured to succeed? Why can't they just be happy with what they have?"

Bapa sighed, his eyes filled with concern. "It's the system, beta. The education system is so competitive, and there's so much pressure to succeed. Students feel like they have to get into the best colleges, get the best jobs, and make their parents proud. But in the process, they forget to take care of themselves.

Mama nodded in agreement. "And it's not just the students, beta. The parents are also to blame. We put so much pressure on our children to succeed, without realizing the impact it has on their mental health."

I felt a pang of guilt, thinking about the pressure Bapa and Mama had put on me to succeed. But I also knew that they had done it out of love and a desire to see me succeed.

"What can we do to change this, Mama?" I asked, feeling a sense of determination.

Mama smiled, her eyes shining with tears. "We can start by being more supportive and understanding, beta. We can encourage our children to pursue their passions, rather than just pushing them to succeed. And we can remind them that it's okay to fail, that it's okay to make mistakes.

Bapa put his hand on my shoulder, his eyes filled with love and pride. "We're proud of you, beta. You're a good kid, and you'll make a great doctor one day."

I smiled, feeling a sense of gratitude towards Bapa and Mama. I knew that they would always be there to support me, no matter what.

My mom shared some wise words that have stuck with me: 'Being successful is not the most important thing in life. What matters most is being a good human being and learning to cope with life's stress.' She reminded me that success may come at different times for different people, but taking care of our mental health and well-being is essential. It's a powerful message that I'll carry with me always.

That day was really tough for me and my family. We were all upset and didn't even check the result or answer key. We just went home and slept, needing time to process our emotions. After a few days, when I was feeling more stable, I finally checked the answer key. I was expecting around 515 marks, which showed that I was starting to feel more confident and prepared to face the outcome.

I was thrilled to see that I had met my expectation of 515 marks, which meant I would likely get a seat in a government medical college! The cut off was around 500, so I was confident that I would make it. I felt an enormous sense of relief and happiness, and I started to enjoy my life again, just like I did the previous year. It was a great feeling to have that weight lifted off my shoulders!"

Waking up in the morning, sipping tea or coffee, and enjoying biscuits was the perfect start to my day. I spent the day relaxing and watching movies in the evening - it was bliss! I literally enjoyed every moment of those thirty days. It was a much-needed break after the exam, and I'm so glad I took the time to unwind and recharge.

When the results were declared, I was anxious to see my score. Although I had aimed for 550, I scored 505 due to two bubbling mistakes on the OMR sheet. But what really surprised me was my rank, which put me on the borderline of getting a seat in a government medical college. I was astonished and confused, unsure of whether I would make it or not. It was a difficult moment, but I'm trying to stay positive and focus on the fact that I've done my best.

During the counseling process, I applied for both state and all-India counseling and waited anxiously for the first round. Unfortunately, I didn't get a college in the first round, which was expected given my rank. However, I was relieved to learn that with my rank, I would likely get a seat in either the second round or the mop-up counseling. It was a stressful time, but I tried to stay positive and focus on the fact that I still had a chance to get a seat.

Both I and my parents were incredibly stressed during those days. It felt like life had put me in a cycle again, where I had to study even harder to get a seat with my current rank. It was a really tough moment for me, and I felt like I was under so much pressure. It was hard to cope with, but I'm trying to stay positive and focus on my goals.

I'm feeling really frustrated and disappointed right now. Students who scored less than me - some even with scores as low as 300 - have got seats in government medical colleges due to quotas. It's hard to see, especially after all the stress and hard work I've put in. But I'm trying to remember that quotas are a part of the system, and it's not a reflection of my worth or abilities. I'll keep moving forward and stay positive.

It's heartbreaking to see someone with less knowledge and capabilities getting a seat in a government medical college, while I, who have more ability and have scored higher, am not getting a seat. It's hard to accept that someone with a score of 300 is getting a seat, while I, who have worked hard and have more knowledge, am not. But I'm trying to stay positive and focus on my strengths. I know I have so much to offer, and there are many paths to success.

I was frustrated to see that over 60% of seats in medical colleges were reserved for SC, ST, and OBC categories. I worry that this may compromise the quality of education and the profession as a whole. I believe that there should be a minimum mark requirement for medical college admission to ensure that students are adequately prepared to become doctors. It's not about hurting anyone, but about maintaining the integrity of the profession and ensuring that patients receive the best possible care. As a general category student, I feel frustrated that my hard work and higher scores are not being recognized.

I had a strong argument with my father about the quota system, but he encouraged me to focus on my studies and scores instead of worrying about the system. My mom intervened and suggested we wait for the mop-up counseling to see what other options are available. I'm trying to stay positive and focus on my goals, knowing that my parents are trying to help me find ways to work within the system. I'm looking forward to the mop-up counseling and exploring other possibilities.

Chapter 10 The Final Showdown

The next morning, after a thoughtful discussion with my parents, I decided to make one final attempt to secure a seat in the medical college. I've come so close, and I don't want to regret not trying again. I've already invested two years in this journey, so why not give it one more shot? I'm willing to take the risk and put in the effort to make my dream a reality. This is my last chance, and I'm determined to make it count!

Honestly, the thought of spending another year trying to get into college was daunting. I felt like I was stuck in limbo, watching my friends move forward with their studies while I was still struggling to get started. Some of my friends were already in their final year of BSc or second or third year of BTech, and I hadn't even taken admission yet. It felt like I was lost at sea, with no direction or clear path forward. I was overwhelmed by the feeling of being left behind and unsure of how to move ahead.

In that moment, I felt like life was unbearable. I thought to myself, 'Have I made a mistake? Should I have chosen a different career path?' I questioned my decision to pursue medical and MBBS, wondering if I was meant to be on this path. I felt like I had done everything right - I worked hard, scored well, and yet, due to quotas and rising cut-offs, I was still struggling to get in. It was like the universe was conspiring against me. I couldn't help but wonder, 'What else could I have done? Is this really where I'm meant to be?

As the months dragged on, I had to wait another year to retake the exam. Time passed slowly, but steadily, and before I knew it, December had arrived again. It was time to fill out the form and take the exam once more. I went through the motions, feeling a mix of frustration and determination. I was determined to succeed this time around, but the wait had taken its toll. I filled out the form, prepared myself, and took the exam again, hoping for a better outcome.

During the end of my preparation, I felt a sense of helplessness wash over me. I realized I had to start all over again, reading and preparing for another year to secure my seat. But then, I received a phone call from my friend Ankita, and her words of encouragement and guidance lifted my spirits. She inspired me to start anew, and I felt a renewed sense of determination to tackle the challenge ahead."

However, I had already completed one year of self-study, and this additional year of self-study seemed even more daunting and traumatic. To hold myself accountable and stay motivated, I turned to my friend Manoj for support. Manoj and I have been friends since Aakash, and we've been through thick and thin together. He's not only one of my closest friends but also a trusted teammate in PUBG Mobile! With his help, I felt more confident and determined to tackle this challenging year ahead.

I fondly remember those late-night gaming sessions with Manoj, where we'd play BGMI or PUBG from 10 pm till 1 or 2 am, after dinner. Those were the days! We'd also study together, and later on, he even became my roommate at Aakash. It's amazing how our friendship evolved over time, from gaming buddies to study partners and eventually, roommates.

During my self-study period, I reached out to Manoj for help and asked him to send me the question papers from Aakash's review tests. I wanted to practice and assess my knowledge, so I had him send the papers to my home. Then, I'd work on them and score decent marks, which boosted my confidence. It was a great way to stay on track and motivated, thanks to Manoj's support!

During my last year of preparation, I faced numerous challenges and mental trauma. The cyclone that hit our area caused significant disruptions, including the postponement of my exam date. Not once, but twice! It was incredibly difficult to maintain my pace and motivation when I had prepared rigorously for a specific date, only to have the exam postponed to a new date. This constant uncertainty took a toll on my mental health, and I struggled to cope with the emotional rollercoaster.

Finally, the exam date arrived, and I was determined to give it my best shot. However, fate had other plans, and I found myself facing the same challenges once again. My exam center was a whopping 50 kilometers away from my hometown, making it a difficult and tiring journey. But I was not going to let that stop me. With a newfound determination, I woke up early that morning, travelled to the center, and arrived just in time to take the exam."

As I made my way to the examination hall, a flurry of thoughts and memories raced through my mind. The entire journey was a poignant flashback of the past two years - the struggles, the heartbreak, the late-night studies, and the unwavering support of my family. I replayed every moment, wondering if I had what it took to succeed. Self-doubt crept in, making me question whether I could do it all again. The cacophony of emotions and memories threatened to overwhelm me, but I steeled myself and pushed forward, determined to face the exam head-on.

Finally, I arrived at my examination seat, took a deep breath, and settled in. I took a sip of water, composed myself, and waited for the question paper to arrive. The examiner handed me the paper and a black ballpoint pen with 'Neat' written on it - a gentle reminder to keep my answers legible! The next three hours flew by in a whirlwind, and before I knew it, I had answered all the questions to the best of my ability. With a sense of relief and accomplishment, I walked out of the examination hall, feeling proud of myself for giving it my all.

As I exited the examination hall, I was greeted by my parents, who were waiting for me outside. They shared a disheartening story about a few students who arrived just five minutes late to the examination center, only to be barred from taking the exam. The thought of those students crying and feeling devastated after waiting an entire year for this opportunity was heart-wrenching. I could deeply empathize with their pain and frustration, and it struck a chord within me. I turned to my father and said..."

"Yes, Papa, I can understand. I've waited three years, and one year felt like an eternity. I can imagine what those students are going through after preparing for a year, only to be denied the chance to appear for the exam because they were just five minutes late. It's heartbreaking. At least they should be allowed to give the exam, but the government's policy is strict in this case. It's not fair, Papa. If they're late by just five minutes, they should still be allowed to appear for the exam. And I said, 'Hope they get a seat next year, Papa.'

"Then, we returned home, and this time, I was exuding confidence. I was convinced that I would secure a seat in medical college. With a sense of assurance, I waited for my results, feeling proud of myself for giving it my all.

And my medical college journey starts with Whispers Through The White Coat.

~ Saswat Abhigyanam

About the Author

Saswat Abhigyanam

Meet Saswat Abhigyanam, a multifaceted individual making a mark in various fields. As a MBBS student, medical influencer, and social activist, He is passionate about making a positive impact on society. Born in 2001, Abhigyanam has always had a vision for creating change and helping others. A talented writer and author, He has explored different genres of writing and has already made a name for in the literary world. An excellent academic student and a visionary, Abhigyanam has won the prestigious PEN IN BOOKS 2024 Young Author Award, a testament to his dedication and talent. With a passion for writing and a commitment to social causes, Saswat Abhigyanam is a rising star in the literary and medical communities.

www.ingramcontent.com/pod-product-compliance
Lightning Source LLC
LaVergne TN
LVHW091228150826
845673LV00003B/1059
* 9 7 8 9 3 6 7 9 5 5 2 9 1 *